Rocket Finds an Egg

All rights reserved. Published in the United States by Random House Studio, an imprint of
Random House Children's Books, a division of Penguin Random House LLC, New York.

Random House Studio with colophon is a trademark of Penguin Random House LLC.

Visit us on the Web!
rhcbooks.com

Educators and librarians, for a variety of teaching tools, visit us at RHTeachersLibrarians.com

Library of Congress Cataloging-in-Publication Data is available upon request.
ISBN 978-0-593-18126-3 (pbk.) — ISBN 978-0-593-18127-0 (trade) —
ISBN 978-0-593-18129-4 (lib. bdg.) — ISBN 978-0-593-18128-7 (ebook)

The text of this book is set in 28-point Century.
The illustrations were digitally rendered.

MANUFACTURED IN CHINA
10 9 8 7 6 5 4 3 2 1
First Edition

Rocket Finds an Egg

Pictures based on the art by Tad Hills

RANDOM HOUSE STUDIO ▲ NEW YORK

It is a sunny day!

Rocket and Bella play
in the meadow.

Rocket stops.

He finds an egg!

It is small, white,
and oval.

Rocket shows Bella.
"We have to find
its home!" Bella says.

Rocket and Bella

search the meadow.

They see Owl.

"Is this your egg?"
Rocket asks.

"No," Owl says.
"My eggs are
all here."

Rocket and Bella
find a bluebird.

The egg is not hers.

Her eggs are blue.

They ask
the little yellow bird.

The egg is too big
to be hers.

The friends ask
a bird with spots.

Her eggs
have spots.

They ask a red bird.

They ask a black bird.

They ask a brown bird.

They can not find
the egg's home!

Rocket and Bella
ask the chickens,
"Is this your egg?"

"No, it is not our egg,"
the chickens say.

At the pond,
the friends ask
the ducks.

The egg is not theirs.

"I am tired,"
Bella tells Rocket.
They take a break.

Then they hear

a <u>SPLASH!</u>

"My egg!"
a turtle says.
"That is my egg!"

"It is a turtle egg,"
Bella says.

"I looked for it
all day,"
the turtle tells them.

"We are glad
you found us!"
Rocket says.

Rocket and Bella
follow the turtle
to her nest.

At last,

the egg is home.